JUMPERS

Things That Move – Climbers
Things That Move – Flyers
Things That Move – Jumpers
Things That Move – Swimmers

Front cover *Leopard frog leaping.*
Back cover *Competition skier in mid-air jump.*

First published in 1991 by
Firefly Books Limited
61 Western Road, Hove
East Sussex BN3 1JD, England

The moral right of the author has been asserted

Editor: Francesca Motisi
Editorial Assistant: Caroline Maw
Designers: Jean and Robert Wheeler

British Library Cataloguing in Publication Data
Powell, Jillian
  Jumpers
  1. Motion
  I. Title   II. Series
  531.11

HARDBACK ISBN 1–85485–102–0

PAPERBACK ISBN 1–85485–171–3

Typeset by DP Press, Limited, Sevenoaks, Kent
Printed and bound by Casterman, S.A., Belgium

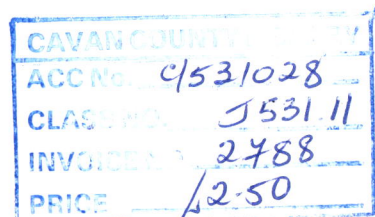

THINGS THAT
MOVE

JUMPERS

Written by Jillian Powell

firefly

Frogs jump by kicking
out their long back legs
and webbed feet. They
can escape from their
enemies by making
big jumps.

Class No. _J.531.11_ Acc No. _4531028._
Author: _Powell-Jillian_ Loc: _/ / SEP 1995_

LEABHARLANN
CHONDAE AN CHABHAIN

1. This book may be kept three weeks. It is to be returned on the last date stamped below.
2. A fine will be charged for every week or part overdue.

Squirrels jump from branch to branch.
They use their long bushy tails to help
them balance.

5

Most whales are very large. They
sometimes jump right out of the water,
using their strong tails.

Monkeys have very long arms and long
fingers which help them to swing and
leap through the trees.

Windsurfers jump when their
board hits a wave!

Long-jumpers run very fast along a track and then jump off a board. They use their arms to help them stay in the air.

Dolphins can jump out of the water, using their strong tails. They jump when they are feeding on fish, showing other dolphins where there is food.

Kangaroos are among the world's best jumpers. They bounce on their long back legs and use their tails to balance.

Impala can run and jump very fast.
They do this to escape from their
enemies like lions and leopards.

Dogs like to jump in play, catching sticks or balls. Some people train their dogs to jump over fences or through hoops in competitions.

The leafhopper (central picture) is a small insect which feeds on plant leaves. It jumps from a leaf before opening its wings to fly.

Fleas (right picture) are tiny insects which live and feed on birds and animals. They have no wings and move by jumping high in the air.

Grasshoppers (left picture) jump to get from one place to another or to escape danger.

Some people ride horses for many different kinds of sport. One of the sports is show jumping. This girl is taking part in a jumping competition.

A parachutist jumps from an aeroplane and opens the parachute by pulling a cord. Like a big umbrella, it helps the parachutist glide down.

Skiers jump into the air when they hit a bumpy bit of snow. They can also enter special ski-jumping competitions.

People can enter a race where they have to jump over hurdles. This sport is called hurdling.

These children are having fun jumping about on a bouncy castle!

Skipping is fun too, and it keeps you fit! You have to jump over the rope when you're skipping.

Any kind of jumping can make you feel good. These children are jumping for joy!

Jumping on a
trampoline is fun.
Make sure a
grown-up is there
to catch you!

Notes for adults

This book teaches children all about the huge variety of creatures that can jump! Stunning photography shows the many jumpers in the human and animal kingdom – from kangaroos and squirrels to long-jumpers and parachutists! Here are some discussion points and questions relating to the pictures.

Discussion points

Page no.

4   Explain why frogs jump (to escape from their enemies by landing in long grass where they are hard to see).

5   Squirrels live in woodland, feeding on nuts, seeds and berries. Some grey squirrels live in towns. Ask the child if s/he has ever seen a squirrel in a park.
10   Explain that dolphins jump when they are feeding on fish, showing other dolphins where there is food. They also jump and somersault in play.
12   Ask the child if s/he remembers why the impala must run and jump very fast.
15   Explain that fleas are very tiny and this photograph is magnified many times. Ask the child if s/he has seen a dog or a cat scratching itself – it's probably got a flea!
17   Explain to the child how a parachute works.
21   Ask the child if s/he likes skipping. Talk about different skipping games and rhymes.

Picture Acknowledgements
The photographs in this book were supplied by: Cephas 8 (John Carter), 20 (Mick Rock); B. Coleman Ltd 5, 7 (inset), 14 (middle), 15 (right) (Kim Tayor); Chris Fairclough 21; Kit Houghton 16; NHPA 11 (Getard Laez), 12 (S Robinson); Oxford Scientific Films *cover* (Stephen Dalton); Tony Stone Worldwide *back cover*, 18 (Adrian Fox), 17 (main pic.) (Peter Lamberti), 19 (Bob Thomas); Topham 9 (Norman Lomax); Timothy Woodcock 22, 23; ZEFA 6, 7, 10, 13, 14 (left), 17 (inset).